I0555728

THREE CELTIC TALES

Also by Moyra Caldecott

FICTION
Guardians of the Tall Stones:
The Tall Stones
The Temple of the Sun
Shadow on the Stones
The Silver Vortex

Weapons of the Wolfhound
The Eye of Callanish
The Lily and the Bull
The Tower and the Emerald
Etheldreda
Child of the Dark Star
Hatshepsut: Daughter of Amun
Akhenaten: Son of the Sun
Tutankhamun and the Daughter of Ra
The Ghost of Akhenaten
The Winged Man
The Waters of Sul
The Green Lady and the King of Shadows
Adventures by Leaf Light and Other Stories

MYTHS AND LEGENDS
Crystal Legends
Women in Celtic Myth
Myths of the Sacred Tree
Mythical Journeys: Legendary Quests

POEMS
The Breathless Pause

AUTOBIOGRAPHY
Multi-dimensional Life

BIOGRAPHY
Oliver Z.S. Caldecott

THREE CELTIC TALES

Moyra Caldecott

Illustrated by Lynette Gusman

Published by
Bladud Books

Copyright © 1999, Moyra Caldecott

Moyra Caldecott has asserted her right under the
Copyright, Designs and Patents Act, 1988, to be
identified as the Author of this work.

First published in 1999 by Mushroom eBooks.

Originally published separately by
Bran's Head Books, as:

Taliesin & Avagddu (1983)
The Twins of the Tylwyth Teg (1983)
Bran, Son of Llyr (1985)

This Edition, with illustrations by Lynette Gusman,
is published in 2007 by Bladud Books, an imprint of
Mushroom Publishing, Bath, BA1 4EB,
United Kingdom

www.bladudbooks.com

All rights reserved. No part of this publication may
be reproduced in any form or by any means without
the prior written permission of the publisher.

ISBN 9781843195481

Contents

Introduction

When the Celtic tribes migrated from central Europe into the British Isles about 700BC they brought with them their rich oral tradition of ancient myths and legends. In the long dark winters, when cattle herding and warfare were difficult, bards told these tales around innumerable hearth fires. Centuries later, they were written down by Christian monks in monastic scriptoriums. In the telling and retelling, changes were often made to suit the individual storyteller, but the essence of the story survived and blazes through to us even today.

The best-known collection of Welsh tales from these early days is commonly known as *The Mabinogion*. Some fragments of these stories were known from the White Book of Rhydderch, *c.*1325, but the earliest comprehensive collection was in the Red Book of Hergest, *c.*1400. Both these versions quote from earlier versions since lost. The Four Branches of the Mabinogion were not translated into English until Lady Charlotte Guest did so in 1849. I find her translation most valuable for its comprehensive and informative section of notes at the back.

Two of the stories in this book are based on texts in Lady Charlotte Guest's translation of *The Mabinogion* published by J M Dent & Co., UK and E P Dutton, New York, 1906. These are "Taliesin and Avagddu" (*pp*.263-285, and notes on *pp*.424-432), and "Bran, Branwen and Evnissyen" (*pp*.33-48 and Notes *pp*.291-297).

"Bran, Branwen and Evnissyen" is the traditional story of the children of Llyr, and how Bran, in death, became a prophet. I have suggested a motive for Evnissyen's destructiveness, and given my own interpretation of the three mysterious doors, as anyone encountering the tale must.

The traditional story of "Taliesin and Avagddu" tells of the transformation of a village lad into the famous bard Taliesin, but says nothing of the fate of Avagddu, the ill-favoured son of Caridwen who was denied the magic potion intended for him. My curiosity as to what happened to Avagddu after he was denied this magic brew inspired me to add suggestions from my own imagination about his fate.

It is well known that the Celts granted a particular importance to the head. Warriors proudly displayed the heads of their honoured enemies as they rode into battle – not only to show that they had conquered that person but that they now had his "power". Sculpted oracle heads are frequently found by archaeologists in Celtic lands. The story of the magical being in human form who challenges the hero to cut off his head and then submit his own to the axe a year later appears many times in Celtic myth and has a deep esoteric meaning. *Sir Gawain and the Green Knight* is perhaps the best known.

"The Twins of the Tylwyth Teg" is based on the story of the Mydfai herdboy mentioned several times in *Celtic Folklore: Welsh and Manx* by John

Rhys (volumes 1 and 2, published by Wildwood House, London 1980 (*pp*.4-15); first published by Oxford University Press, 1901). In this story we are only given the life of the one twin, Olwen, and are told only what happened to her when she entered the world of mortal man above the surface of the lake. But whatever happened to the second twin? And what went on beneath the lake? In this retelling of the traditional tale, these questions are given an answer. The story of Haelwyn, the rejected twin, is a new addition of my own based on clues in the original story.

Bran, Branwen and Evnissyen

Over the sea came the long boats from Ireland, satin flags flying, warriors with shields upside down to show that this was a peaceful mission: their king, Matholwch, was seeking the daughter of Llyr, the beautiful Branwen, to share his throne and his bed.

The High King of Britain, Bendigeidfran, Bran the Blessed, the giant son of Llyr, brother of Branwen, greeted them graciously.

"Two such kingdoms," he said, "should be at peace with one another. Come sister, see what you think of this man, this king of Ireland."

Branwen, dark hair bound with river pearls, gown of sapphire blue... Llyr's daughter, as beautiful as the sea at dawn, stood behind the broad shoulder of her brother and peeped out at the man from across the sea.

She saw that he was shorter than her brother – but then, who was not? For no man on earth could match Bran's height. Matholwch was auburn haired. There was gold at his shoulder holding the green folds of his cloak. There were golden torcs at his throat and on his arms. His boots were laced with silk. He looked at her steadily: his eyes grey and smiling, curious, but admiring. There was a rustle among the ladies of the court... a whisper... a smile... Matholwch of Ireland was a handsome man. Old women who are wiser than young ones might say he was too handsome. "There is a prettiness to him," one whispered to another. "A weakness… He will be easily led." "No bad thing for the Princess then," was the reply, "for she will be able to rule the land through him." The first shook her head. "Not good," she said. "Too vain. Look at the embroidery on his shirt… His hands are too white… his hair is too curled and perfumed…" "Look at those thighs," the young women whispered, "that chest… that smile…"

Branwen was caught in the net of his smile and touched her brother shyly on the arm.

Bran looked fondly down at her. Almost imperceptibly she nodded and smiled, and then ducked behind him to hide her blushes.

"Let my sister be the seal on the peace between us," Bran said smiling, holding out his arms to his new brother. Every man in the hall beat palm upon leather arm-guard or stamped his foot; every woman clapped and laughed. Branwen's friends hugged her close. Not one but wished the handsome Prince was theirs.

Then began the feasting and the celebration. A mighty auroch horn of mead was passed from King to King, and then to brother, noble, kinsman and companion.

Branwen's women took her away and decked her in jewels and flowers.

When she returned, she sat at the feet of her new lord and played upon the harp. Her voice was as clear as the silver water that falls from mountain top to secret forest pool, as joyful as a bird at dawn, as fine as the gold thread of a goldsmith…

All listened enraptured to the song of a young girl in love.

Bran watched and listened benignly, and when she was done he himself took the harp and played a stronger lay. He sang of love between peoples, not just between a man and a woman. He sang of differences between peoples that could be used for peace and not for war. He sang of life and strength and joy and there was no mention in all his song of killing or of hate. He finished with a song specially for Branwen and honoured her as a golden bridge between two great lands.

But the mischief maker, the shadow spinner, the knave of darkness is never far away.

Bran had two half-brothers, Nissyen and Evnissyen: light and dark, the peace-maker and the strife-maker. In Bran's heart these two each had a place.

Evnissyen, returning from a hunting expedition, found that the Princess, his half sister, was wed, and without his consent.

Since childhood Evnissyen had brooded: bitter that Bran, his half-brother, was loved by all. When Bran walked into a room the faces of all those present lit up. When he spoke everyone listened, nodded and smiled. When Evnissyen entered a room a shadow fell, people turned shoulders to him, and murmured among themselves. He was a warrior, but Bran always outran him, threw spear further, flashed sword faster. Nissyen, his twin, did not bother him as much as Bran did. For Nissyen offered no competition. He was a gentle poet, a

weaver of garlands for ladies, a singer of songs. But Bran was everything Evnissyen wanted to be – powerful and mighty – much honoured and loved.

Bran, seeing how Evnissyen resented him, tried to allay the boy's antagonism, spoke fait to him, assured him that he was valued in every way within the family of Llyr. As Evnissyen grew to manhood he was included in family consultations, family decisions, though more often than not his wishes were overridden by the rest. But this time he was not even consulted. Branwen, his beautiful half-sister, the light of his life, who always smiled at him when others frowned, who rocked him in her arms when he was ill, and played fidchell with him when he was well, was being sent away across the sea, married to a stranger without even a word to him.

A black storm gathered in his heart. He would put a stop to this! No stranger would violate his sister. No man would take her away from him without his agreement. He would show them who was the real power in the family!

He said nothing to his kinsmen, but, white with rage, stormed out of the great hall, through the noisy yard where the carts that had brought food for the feasting were being reloaded with the chests and boxes and baskets that the new Queen wanted to take with her, and out onto the hillside where the Irish King's horses were peacefully grazing.

For no more than a few moments he stared at them before he hatched his cruel vengeance.

"Insult for insult," he murmured and drew the dagger at his side.

The horses screamed as he maimed them and his

arms were running blood when, tight-lipped and head held high, he strode back through the yard and disappeared into the castle.

No time was lost in bringing the news to Matholwch, his companions crowding him with gory details and clamouring for vengeance.

Bewildered by the savage insult of one brother and the fair treatment of the other, Matholwch withdrew in haste to his ships, waiting in readiness on the shore. Branwen, weeping, was given no time to bid farewell to her family and friends, but was taken roughly, more hostage than bride.

Then came the horror of those at Bran's court who saw what Evnissyen had done. No pride would have been felt had the deed been done against an enemy, and against a friend… the shame was un-bearable.

Bran at once sent his brother Manawyddan and his best men to offer atonement. Each horse was to be replaced and the Irish King was to be given a staff of silver as tall as himself and a plate of gold as wide as his face.

Matholwch hesitated. Matholwch considered. Branwen waited at his side anxiously. The compan-ions murmured in his ear that the compensation was not enough.

"You insult me further with your silver and gold," he said haughtily. "Give me the Prince Evnissyen's head to carry back to Ireland and I might forgive the House of Llyr."

"That is not possible my lord," Manawyddan said quietly. "The Prince Evnissyen is my brother's brother and the shedding of his blood cannot be undertaken honourably. But what say you to a cauldron into which the bodies of men who have been slain in battle on one day may be thrown to emerge, on the next, ready to fight again?"

Manawyddan had been instructed not to offer this unless there was no hope of peace between the two nations without it. To give it to another man was the greatest act of trust anyone could contemplate.

Matholwch and his companions were silent and then withdrew to consult. When they returned, the Irish king agreed to return to Bran's court to negotiate the matter of compensation.

Then was a feast prepared that outdid even the wedding feast, and Bran, the High King of the Island of the Mighty, spoke to Matholwch, the High King of Ireland, about the cauldron he would give.

"Note," he said, "that I give it to you to be held in trust but never to be used. The warriors that emerge from the cauldron may kill, but they will not know why they kill. They may walk, but they may not know where they walk. They are capable of neither thought, nor talk, and he who unleashes them on the world will rue the day. I give it to you only to prove my trust in you and to prove that you may trust me."

"But they do kill?" asked the companions of Matholwch eagerly.

"Yes," said Bran. He was thinking that in all the years he had had the cauldron he had not made use of it – and now he was letting it out of his hands. It was the measure of the value he put on peace be-

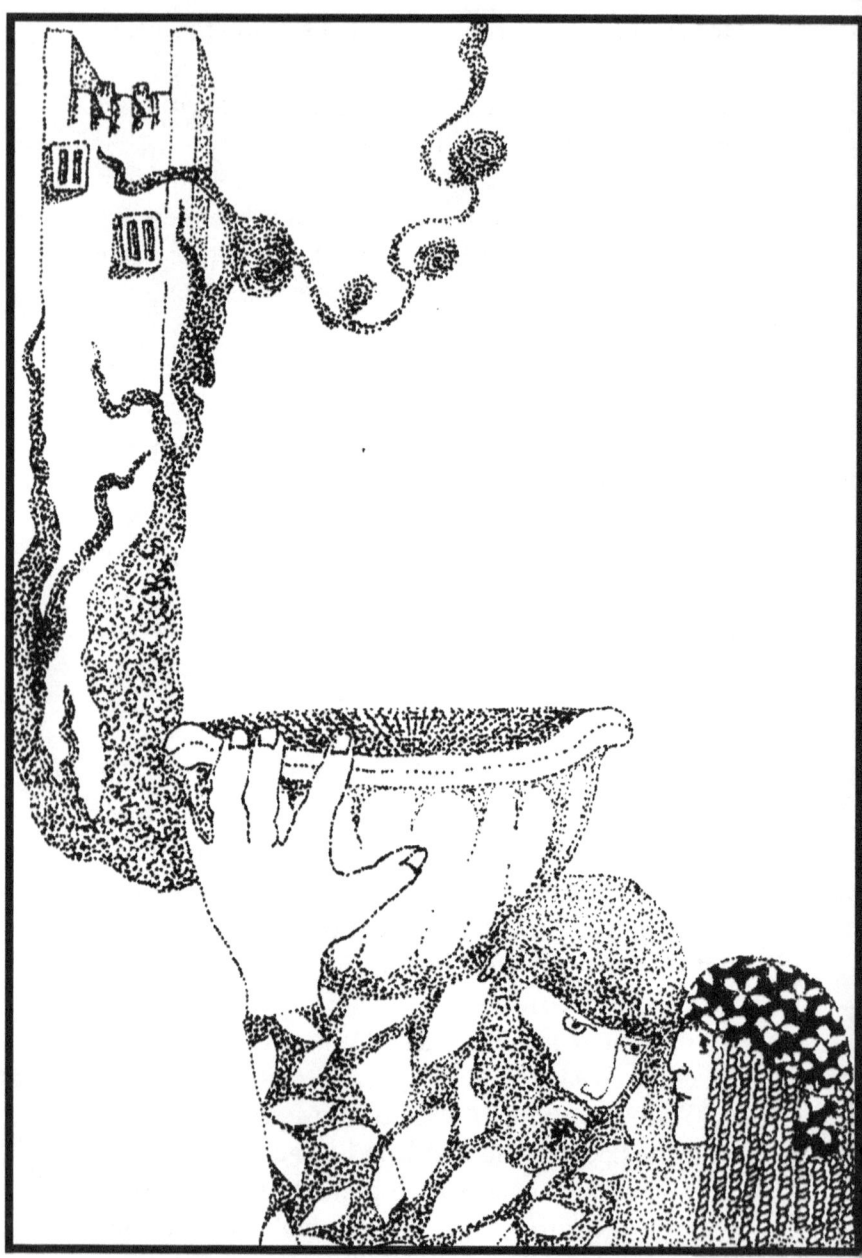

tween the two nations that he was prepared to let it go: and it was the measure of his trust that he felt so little fear as he did so.

"This cauldron," said Matholwch thoughtfully during the second night of feasting. "How did you come by it?"

"I received it from a couple who came from Ireland. They told me how they had escaped from an Iron House which had been made white hot around them."

"I know this couple," the King of Ireland said. "They caused me great harm. I invited them to my court because they claimed that the wife could bear a son in six weeks, who, at the end of another six weeks, could be a warrior fully armed. I thought to strengthen my kingdom with such warriors: but instead they caused me nothing but trouble. They grew so strong and dangerous I was at my wits end to know how to be free of them. At length I trapped them in an Iron House and tried to destroy them with fire."

Bran then told him how he had received them hospitably and given them a place in his kingdom, and they, in gratitude, had given him the cauldron.

"Who holds this cauldron," the companions whispered to Matholwch, "has complete power. No one will ever attack us while we hold it."

"But..." said Matholwch, remembering the mindless warriors who had all but destroyed his kingdom from within once before.

"Take it!" the companions urged. "If Bran has it we will always be at his mercy."

Matholwch listened to their counsel and accepted the cauldron. "I swear," he said sincerely to Bran, "I will hold it, but I will never use it."

In thirteen ships the King of Ireland sailed back to his country with his fair Queen at his side, and for a year there was peace and happiness as the people honoured the daughter of Llyr. There was not one who came to her court that left without a gift.

At the end of the year she gave birth to a young prince, and they called him Gwern, son of Matholwch. Branwen held him close in her arms and knew that he was more precious than all the jewels in the world. But it was the custom in those times to give the infants of the royal family out to fosterage and she was parted from her son.

This was the beginning of her sorrows.

By the second year of their marriage the King's closest companions began to murmur among themselves that the young Queen was beginning to have too great an influence, not only on the King but on the ruling of the land. The people loved her and there were times when petitioners came to her rather than to the King, and sometimes decisions were made by her while he was away hunting. Her brother Bran had always treated her with as much respect as he did her brothers, and many a time in council it had been her voice that was heard above the others. Now, lonely without her son, she devoted herself to the people of her adopted land. This did not please the nobles around the King, and they soon pointed out to him with sly and persistent whispering that the country was being ruled by the House of Llyr through Branwen, and not by Matholwch the King. Then they reminded him that, no matter how much compensation had been paid, he had still been insulted by the royal house of Llyr in the matter of the maimed horses.

"Insult for insult," they whispered. "Her family mock you even now for your weakness in forgiving when you should have sought vengeance, and in allowing a woman, one of their women, to rule your kingdom."

So at last, on their advice, but against the prompting of his own heart, he took his wife and forbade her rightful place in his bed and at his court. She was sent to work in the kitchens of the castle, the recipient of constant blows and insults.

"That way," said the King's companions, "she will learn humility and you will show the country that it is ruled by the house of Matholwch and not of Bran."

For three years Branwen suffered and for three years all communications were broken off with mainland Britain.

She looked at the wide, wide sky that covered both her husband's land and the land of her father and sang this song:

"Ah, sun that shines
on the one and the many
hear my lament!
He who listens to whispering
has turned against me.
He who loves me

has turned from me.
He who is king
has left me.
The one is swayed by the many
and the many has no heart."

As she scrubbed iron pots in the dark and airless kitchen she thought of the mountains of her homeland, the mist whirling away before the winds, the sound of water falling from rock to rock... magical rowan trees scarlet with berries, and forests of birch and oak, lush with fern and moss... She thought of the lakes, silver mirrors reflecting the sky one moment and the next, turned to dark slate-grey as a breeze sprang up. She longed to hear the soft whispering and singing of the reeds at the water's edge. She longed to hear the deep but gentle voice of her brother Bran.

Her only friend during this long wearisome time was a starling who came to her for kitchen scraps. Patiently she taught it to speak her name, and at the end of three years she sent it to her brothers with a message bound to its ankle.

Buffeted by wind and storm it fought its way across the Irish Sea and landed at last, bedraggled and out of breath, on the broad shoulder of Bran. Not at first realising what it was he brushed it off impatiently, but, as it fell, he noticed that it was a small bird near to death. Gently he picked it up and cradled it in his huge hand. As it lay there, heart pounding, he fancied he heard it speak his sister's name. Puzzled, he leant down to hear more clearly and noticed a small piece of vellum attached to its ankle. Again the bird spoke the name of Branwen. Then in astonishment all crowded round the tiny bird. Bran fed it and soothed it and as it recovered its strength the sweet sound of Branwen's name trilled more and more readily from its beak. Carefully Bran unwound the strip of vellum from its ankle and read aloud to all his court the sad tale told there.

In this way the sons of Llyr heard of their sister's plight.

Bran, the High King, called a council and it was agreed that Branwen should be rescued. Seven princes under the command of Caradwac, his son, should remain to hold the kingdom safe, while the rest should follow Bran to Ireland. The names of the seven were: Caradwac the son of Bran; Heveydd Hir; Unic Glew Ysgwyd; Iddic the son of Anarawc Gwalltgrwn; Fodor the son of Ervyll. Gwlch Minascwrn; and Llassar the son of Llaesar Llaesgygwyd.

Like a forest crossing the ocean the masts of Bran's ships put fear into the hearts of Matholwch and his men.

His companions at once advised Matholwch to retreat to the other side of a great river and destroy the bridge that spanned it. But Bran, the giant, coming to the river, spoke to his companions and said: "He who would be a chief must also be a bridge." He laid his great bulk down across the water and became a bridge for his men to cross. So mighty was the force that crossed that day that Matholwch and his men knew that they could not withstand it.

Messengers were sent to sue for peace.

They offered that Gwern, the son of Branwen, should immediately be given the throne of Ireland in recompense for what had been done to her. But Bran was not satisfied with this. The boy was too young to rule. The companions then advised Matholwch to offer Bran the kingdom to be held in trust for Branwen's son, and, as a token of their King's good will, a castle was to be built for Bran the giant, so big that even he could dwell in it with comfort. Branwen was pleased with this offer and Bran agreed to accept it for the sake of peace.

The companions of Matholwch the King went away smiling: but the smile was not from the heart.

The castle was built and the great feast day arrived when Bran should take up residence as Regent of Ireland.

Evnissyen, ever suspicious, insisted on examining the building before his brother entered. He found leather bags hanging from all the columns of the Great Feast Hall.

"What do these contain?" he demanded.

"Meal," he was told. "Food for the new King."

"Ah," said Evnissyen, "good meal, I hope," and he squeezed the bag as though to test the meal. He smiled grimly as he felt a man's skull crack between his fingers.

It was not until he had dealt with all the bags thus that he allowed Bran to enter the castle.

At the feast in celebration Branwen's son Gwern took his place at court for the first time and stood proudly before his kin.

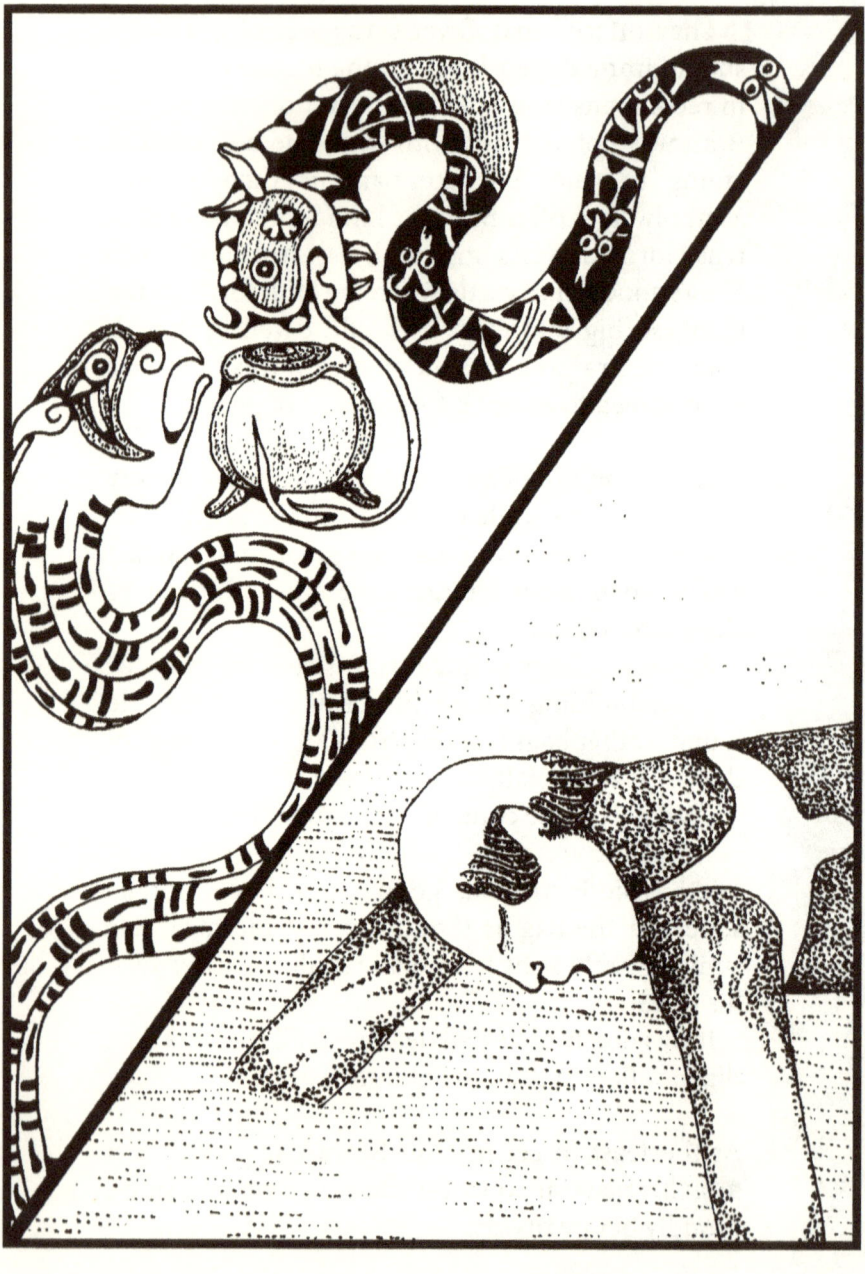

He bowed before them one by one, speaking words of honour and greeting – but he did not come to Evnissyen as quickly as Evnissyen would have liked. Bitterly, the man watched as the boy greeted his brother Nissyen, and he brooded on what he took to be yet another insult. It was when the young lad inadvertently bowed to a minor kinsman before he reached his uncle that Evnissyen could bear it no longer. Veins stood out upon his neck as his body tensed with ungovernable rage. He clenched and unclenched his fists, and then, when the lad at last came to him, he seized his slight form and flung it bodily into the fire – shouting that he'd be insulted by no spawn of Matholwch.

Screaming, Branwen would have leapt after her son had not Bran held her tight against his side, his shield over her, as every man reached for his weapons and a roar that was the end of peace rocked the hall.

Then was there war between the two lands.

As day by day the fighting grew fiercer, the companions of Matholwch reminded him of the cauldron, and, although he knew that to use it might unleash forces he would not be able to control, the temptation to do so was too much for him. At last he kindled a fire under the cauldron, and every warrior that was slain was thrown in to rise again the next day.

Mindlessly they fought: looking neither to the left nor to the right. Killing was all they knew and killing was all they did.

Bran's force could do nothing against them.

On the third day the gentle Nissyen raised his shield to fend off a blow from one of the companions of Matholwch, and in one of those strange long moments when everything seems extraordinarily clear, he saw, over his enemy's shoulder, one of the walking dead approaching. Horrified he watched the dead man raise its dagger arm and realised that it was aimed at the Irish warrior and not himself. "So," he thought, "he who uses the cauldron will be destroyed as surely as he against whom it is used." He dropped his shield and seized his fellow human being with a sudden desperate strength and flung him aside. "Don't you see," he cried, "we will both…" But he fell to the dead man's dagger before he could utter another word. The Irish warrior, fallen but unharmed, stared uncomprehendingly at Bran's brother lying dead at his feet.

And then Evnissyen, seeing what he had wrought and that his act was bringing about the destruction of his whole family and his entire nation, began to think how he could mend the situation. Every night he watched how the Irish dead were gathered up from the battlefield and how every morning they were there to fight again. He knew that unless the cauldron was destroyed there could be no hope for any of them.

One night after the fiercest of the battles, he dressed himself in the blood-soaked clothes of an Irish warrior and lay among the dead. His limbs hung limp as he was lifted and flung on the pile of bodies in the cauldron. Though his gorge rose at the limbless, headless corpses, he lay still until the very last one was thrown on top of him... until he heard the crackle of the flames... until he felt the heat of the iron against his flesh. Then he saw a finger move on one of the dead and knew that he could afford to wait no longer: already the bodies were beginning to revive. Pouring with sweat he stretched his limbs as far as they would go, wedging his feet against one side of the cauldron, his hands against the other. He strained with every muscle in his body... strained until the pain in every part of him was unbearable... but still the iron held. Then did Evnissyen cry out and in the cry was all the regret for his false pride, his rage, his spite... and in that cry was his love for his brother Bran. In that moment the iron split... cracked... fell apart... pouring into the flames the lifeless bodies of the warriors and with them Evnissyen, the half-brother of Bran. The heart in his breast cracked like the cauldron, spilling its life's blood on Irish soil.

So did Evnissyen pay in some part for the evil that he had done.

Seven only of Bran's mighty force escaped alive. And five only of the Irish. The country was devastated: no crops grew: no birds sang...

Bran himself was wounded in the foot by a poisoned arrow and knew that his life was over. He called the seven to his side – Pryderi, Manawyddan, Gluneu Eil Tarn, Taliesin, Ynawc, Grudyen the son of Muryel, and Heilyn the son of Gwynn Hen – and commanded that they should cut off his head and

bear it to Llandin, the sacred hill, the White Mount in Londinium, and bury it there, with its face towards Gaul.

"While it is buried there," he said, "no enemy will conquer the land. But first the journey must be as I say. Listen well and follow my instructions carefully. Stay seven years in Harlech and listen to the birds of Rhiannon. I will speak with you as I did when I was alive, and all will be pleasant and comfortable between us. When it is time to leave you must stay four score years at Gwales in Penvro and I will speak with you there. There will be a castle and in the Great Hall will be three doors. Two you may open: but the third must be kept shut. If ever this door is opened my speech will cease and you must hurry to Londinium to bury my head. Mark well, and obey."

Then the seven did as he bid them and set off for their homeland with Bran's head carried between them: Branwen, his sister, mourning, at their side.

But in their absence Bran's old kingdom had been taken by Caswallawn's sword and the seven princes he had left in charge were dead. Even Caradwac his son.

Branwen thought about all that had happened and she could face life no longer.

Where lie you now, Lady of Sorrow? Still where they buried you in a four-sided grave by Alaw's willow woven bank on the sad isle of Anglesey? Or do you sing still to anyone who will listen that one heart speaks truer than the whispers of the heartless many?

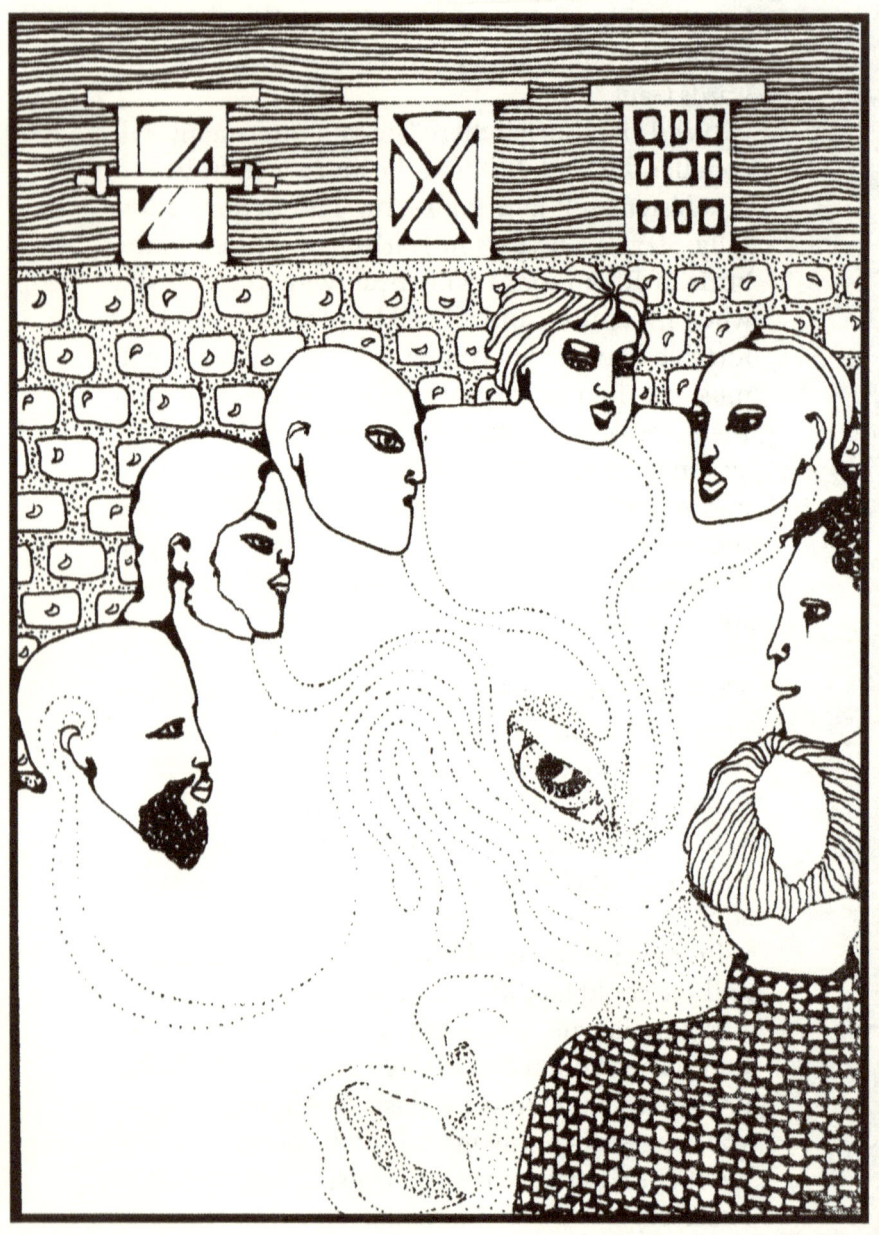

* * *

On Harlech rock the seven made their stay. Beneath them the silver waters of the bay lay quietly, half ringed by shimmering distant blue mountains. Bran's head was their companion.

He spoke to them of war and he spoke to them of peace, and in all the speaking one thing was clear: no peace will hold in the world if it is not rooted in an understanding heart.

He spoke to them of times when everything seemed lost: yet everything was gained; and he spoke to them of times when everything seemed gained, yet everything was lost.

He spoke to them of heroes who won all that they needed to win without shedding a drop of blood.

He spoke to them of love and he spoke to them of hate and in all the speaking one thing was clear: he who hates, destroys himself before he destroys his enemy: and he who loves gains more than he gives.

From across the silver sea three birds sang of life, and the life they sang of had no end and no beginning: "the body is a seamless garment... and the individual soul is a bird of passage... but the spirit," sang the birds, "the spirit lives forever... Yes! the spirit lives forever... It cannot be seen, because it is the Eye that sees."

The singing was the most beautiful that they had ever heard and it continued day and night without ceasing, though sometimes they were aware of it and sometimes they were not.

At the end of seven years they felt that no more

time had passed than seven days and seven nights, yet they knew that it was time for the next stage of their journey.

Quietly they left the place and went to Gwales in Penvro. There they found a castle overlooking the ocean and there they settled with the head of Bran.

In the spacious hall within this castle where they set about their feasting were three doors.

Outside the castle, four score years went by, but within, no time passed at all.

Bran spoke to them of the rise and fall of kingdoms and in all the speaking one thing was clear: no kingdom rose that did not fall. He spoke of lies and truth and flattery: of subterfuge and treachery; and told them that he who understood himself, understood others: that he who did not fool himself could not be fooled by others: that the same eyes must be used to look both at self and foe.

Through one door they passed to gaze upon the past and sing the songs of their fathers.

Through the second they came upon a hall of extraordinary mirrors by which they were enabled to see not only their outward forms, but all the planes of Being within…

But the third door was never opened.

They feasted on nightingales and saffron, on honey wine and parsley bread.

They sang and spoke and rested: and in all things their mighty King was their cheerful companion… but one question he would not answer, and that was why they should not open the third door.

One suggested that it might be a vision of the world's future so disturbing that they would not be able to restrain themselves from rushing out to try to change it. Another, that it might be a vision of the Blessed Isles of the Dead so beautiful that they might want to leave this life at once to journey there... or so frightening they might fall into despair.

At last Heilyn, the son of Gwynn, could bear it no longer, and opened the third door. For a moment, after all their speculation, they could not believe that what they were seeing was no more than the ordinary world they had left behind. They saw farmers ploughing the land, they saw roads crowded with people hurrying to market, they saw trees bending in the wind...

Suddenly their castle seemed constricting and they longed to walk on the roads among people again.

They looked at the head of Bran, and they could not believe that it had spoken to them. The flesh was beginning to slough off and the eyes were dead and glassy. Hastily they wrapped it in a cloak and carried it as quickly as they could to Londinium, where they buried it as Bran had requested, beneath Llandin, the sacred mound.

As they turned to go their separate ways, the companionship of Bran's head seemed like a fading dream, a beautiful interlude of mystical contemplation, that bore no relation to real life.

They began lives of action, of change, of movement, almost ashamed that they had so long avoided this. Sometimes Bran's wisdom shaped their decisions, informed their actions: but sometimes they failed him and failed themselves. Perhaps, they thought, Bran had meant them to open the third door all along and return to the ordinary world – but only when they were ready. He knew that they could not sustain the heights of understanding necessary to absorb all his teaching while they were caught up in the noisy confusion of everyday life. Because of Heilyn's ungovernable curiosity they had opened the third door too soon and had come back to the world only half prepared, wasting the wisdom Bran had sought to teach them.

Sadly, at the end of long lives, the seven returned to the mound and knelt beside their old companion.

Then did Bran's head speak again.

By Arthur's time, Bran's head had lain for centuries beneath the Holy Hill, while pilgrims had come from far and wide to consult it as oracle or ask for healing. Many were the miracles that were reported from the place, and many a wise decision was made under its guidance. In his youth Merlin himself sought teaching from the head, and was among those who journeyed every year at the winter solstice to celebrate Bran's victory over death…

The head became many things to many people: some murmured that Bran had been the first to bring Christianity to this land and that it was in Christ's power that his head still prophesied and healed. Others that he had been an ancient god, son of Llyr, the Sea God, denied by the Christians, yet still prophesying and healing in the mighty tradition of the ancient times. Whatever the form their belief took, the head still spoke to them, for it was speaking to the deep levels within the human heart where the true spirit abides.

In all the years since the time Bran's seven companions had buried his head, the land had been more or less peaceful: the Romans had withdrawn, leaving the people to go about their daily business. The belief that Bran's head was guarding them from harm was very strong.

But the earth is restless. Not only do the rocks move, the rivers change their courses, and whole continents slip and slide, but the little creatures on its surface who cluster together in their millions, jostling for position among themselves, even though there is enough room for all of them, sometimes burst out and move en masse to occupy another place.

Such a moment came during the reign of Arthur.

From across the sea the Germanic tribes – the Angles and the Saxons and the Jutes – came sailing up the eastern rivers and round the southern coast, sails billowing, warriors drumming on their shields.

In terror and despair many rushed to the shrine of Bran and demanded a magic thunderbolt... a host of avenging ravens...

Quietly and calmly, gazing across the centuries, Bran prophesied a nation which gained its strength not from the purity of its blood but from the strengths of many nations working together within it…

And then Arthur rose and came to the White Mound, the Holy Hill gleaming with its white quartz covering.

"Bran," he said, "mighty king of old. The people turn to you expecting you to provide a miracle to save us from the foe. They do nothing to protect themselves, but call on you, invoking your ancient magic, your legendary power. I am a warrior and I rely on my own strong arm to defend myself against the enemy – I am Arthur, King!"

"See," he said to his distraught people, "this old skull has no magic power to save you."

And he had the ancient head dug up.

"Throw it in the river," he said, "and let the tide take it where it will."

Horrified, the people stood beside the river gazing at the spot where their holy relic, their powerful talisman, had entered the water. They expected some sign, some great portent… perhaps they thought Arthur would be struck down for his act of sacrilege.

But nothing happened. The water closed over its new burden as it had closed over all others. The tide ran strong, the tide ran deep…

Arthur rallied the people to war and fought with his strong arm and the strength of his warriors. Many battles were lost, many good men killed or maimed, before at last, at Baden Mount, he made the stand that held, briefly – only briefly – the Saxon advance.

Sometimes, even today, Bran's voice can he heard as the tide washes over his skull, and priests standing in the great Cathedral that rose upon the holy mound pray for the souls of their enemies as sincerely as they pray for the souls of their friends.

Sometimes, even today, a voice in a country grown strong with the strength of many nations, pleads for understanding and not suspicion; wisdom and not weapons…

Taliesin and Avagddu

Lady Caridwen, Earth Mother, skin like new leaves in spring, eyes brown as the roots of the cosmic-tree, hair of flame, what do you see when you wait for your third child beside the lake of Tegid? Son and daughter have you, beautiful as forest and mountain; the third must surpass them, the third is your greatest wish, your heart's desire. You will call his name "Man" when he is born; "Avagddu" when he has taken his first suck; "the right hand of the High King" when he has grown to manhood.

But the day that he is born the sun does not shine, the birds do not sing. He lies between your legs like a stone, like a wrinkled and rotting fruit. He looks at you with vacant eyes and you know that among the beings of the Great God's creation he is an aberration.

Keening, you rock him in your arms: keening, your love for him is undiminished.

"He will be beautiful," you sing. "He will be strong! He will be wise!"

The Lady Caridwen seeks the advice of priests and scholars, consults the books of the Fferyllt, and decides to boil a cauldron of Inspiration and Knowledge for her son that he may one day so surpass all men in wisdom and the art of prophecy that no one will notice his ugliness. Carefully she gathers herbs according to the cunning of the astrologers and sorcerers she has consulted, each plucked from the earth at the rising or the zenith or the setting of the planets and of the moon, each holding the influence of the particular moment, each an invisible thread in the web of the universe. One by one she gathers them and sets them in the cauldron, each following each to bring new influence, to bring new virtue to the brew. She chants their names and the secret relationships between them that only the great sages know. All the wisdom of the ancients she puts into the cauldron and all the wisdom that is yet to be... the Three Names of God... the Names of the Spirits of Light and the Names of the Spirits of Dark... the secret code by which crystals form or the seed in the woman grows... not herself knowing the Whole Design she feeds in the essence of All that Is...

At one side of the cauldron she sets a blind man named Morda to chop wood and keep the fire kindled beneath it; at the other side she sets a young lad, Gwion Bach, the son of Gwreang of Llanfair in Caereinion, Powys, to keep it stirred. A Year and a Day must pass before the brew will be ready and in all that time nothing must interrupt the boiling and the bubbling. A year of summer and autumn, winter and spring, and beyond this, a day that is out of Time. At the end of this only three drops of the liquid must be swallowed. Three drops will give the inspiration and all the wisdom a man can absorb: one more drop will destroy him.

Impatiently the Great Lady waits... impatiently she watches... her son Avagddu an abomination in the sight of men...

* * *

Gwion stirs, weary of stirring: his playmates play: his father's cattle are unattended. Day by day he stirs and the ladle grows heavier, the cauldron grows fuller, and the magic brew thicker. On the last day, when his arm is aching, his back is breaking, and his eyes are blurred for lack of sleep, a bubble on the surface bursts and three drops fly off and scald his finger.

Instinctively he puts it to his mouth, and sucks.

Instantly Time stops, the Tree of Life bursts into blossoms of fire: from the Beginning to the End Gwion sees what Was and Is and Shall Be. For a moment he crouches, stunned, not realising what is happening, his mind expanded beyond the Universe to See what has never been seen before... to dream what never has been dreamed... Words richer than the jewels in a king's ransom form on his tongue, but even they cannot express the beauty and the magnificence of what he sees in that moment... the Great Design... the Meaning beyond meaning...

But the beauty of the Whole is not all he sees... he sees pain before its transformation... and he sees his own immediate danger from the Lady Caridwen. What should have been the gift to her son has been given to a common village lad. Her anger will be greater than thunder in the mountains, lightning on the high peaks, flooding in the valleys...

He drops the ladle and flees...

The cauldron rumbles as the liquid over-boils... the sides crack, the now poisonous potion roars

down the hillside, scalding and destroying every-thing in its path. The horses in the field below, whinnying with fear, are trapped and lie flounder-ing in its wake, to die slowly…

The Lady Caridwen, knowing the brew is almost ready, had gone to fetch her ill-favoured son. She returns to see what havoc has been wrought… what waste… She sees the shards of the broken cauldron, the burnt and shrivelled grass. She sees the blind man cowering beside the pile of wood. She seizes a tree trunk and clubs him on the head, screaming invective. Sobbing, he tells her he is innocent…

Then she looks for Gwion, and to her his absence proves his guilt. Shrieking curses on his head she sets off in pursuit, her hair streaming out behind her like whips of fire, her eyes like burning coals…

Seeing her coming Gwion changes himself into a hare and springs across the sward, distancing him-self with every bounce and bound…

"Ay-e-e-e-e!" she howls, the wind in her nose, her ears as keen as a hound's.

Heart thumping Gwion knows he is pursued and knows that death will be brutal and bloody. All that a hare knows he knows… but as a man who has drunk of the Cauldron of Caridwen he knows more.

The river bank with willows is before him, the water running deep and wide. He changes into a fish and leaps the white of the rapids, darts and gleams and swims… But behind him comes Caridwen, the otter bitch, sliding through the wa-ter, curving with the water's curve, shadow-grey beneath the surface, eyes relentless, fixed…

All that a fish knows he knows… but as a man

who has drunk of the Cauldron of Caridwen he knows more.

He leaps, and as the air touches his silver scales, fills his lungs, his body transforms to bird and wings away, drops of water falling from his feathers.

Filled with air and light, rejoicing, he soars and coasts, sees the land far below… jagged cliffs and hill tops, slopes of green, and forested valleys, tiny villages with plumes of hearth-smoke…

Across his shining vision falls a shadow. Eye-bright he turns his head… and sees Caridwen the hawk about to swoop.

Fear-filled he twists and turns a downward spiral, her beak and claws reaching for him, the thudding of her wings close upon his back…

All that a bird knows he knows… but as a man who has drunk of the Cauldron of Caridwen he knows more.

He spies a heap of winnowed wheat on a thresh-ing floor and drops upon it, changing in the instant to one of the grains.

Black beating shadows of the hawk's wings scat-ter the grain far and wide, but she cannot find him.

He believes himself safe at last… until… mighty hawk to barnyard hen she feeds on the grain… peck, pecking, nearer all the time, scratching with her feet, tossing the wheat hither and thither.

All that a seed knows he knows… but as a man…

This time, he is too slow, and she swallows him before he can change.

In her dark body he lies for nine months. The earth turns, the moon waxes and wanes, the sun grows faint and strong again.

For nine months she waits in hate for his re-birth.

In Spring, on the day of readiness, he slides from her body as her son Avagddu had done, but when she looks at him with knife raised to kill, she cannot do it, for he is beautiful beyond anyone she has ever seen, wise with the knowledge of all that is in the earth and all that is above it, his eyes the eyes of a Seer, his tongue the tongue of a poet... weeping, she wraps him in a leather bag and throws him into the sea.

The day she does this is the 29th day of April.

Green water, rising and falling like the breast of a mother... primeval ocean... spirit-pool... God's womb...

To all depths swims the Fish in the Ocean of Consciousness... with the child following... the child following.

Night is dark and stars pierce the water with needles of light.

But dawn comes...

Ah, yes, dawn comes.

On the thirtieth day of April, the eve of May, Elphin the son of Gwyddno is watching at his father's fishing weir on the beach between Dyvi and Aberystwyth. The sea rolls in over what had once been his father's fertile fields, before the dyke that held it back had broken. Elphin had not himself witnessed that dreadful night when the drunk sea-guard had failed to report the breach, but his father's lamentations and curses are famous among the villages:

"A cry from the sea awakens me this night!
A cry from the sea arises above the winds!
Accursed be the watcher who watches not!
Who brings desolation to my lands
And mourning to the people of the low lands."

Gwyddno's great riches are gone, but the fishing weir brings in a good living. On May eve in particular the weir-ward usually takes a hundred pounds or more. This year Elphin has been given the privilege of it for the one day. He is newly wed but has no substance on which to found his household. His father and his father's friends believe he was born under an ill-fated star, for nothing he tries goes well and his ways are so slow and gentle, his movements and speech so awkward, it is a wonder any maid has been found for him.

The day passes and for once in all the years the weir yields nothing. Elphin dreads his return home empty handed, believing that his father will blame him for the bad luck that has befallen them this day.

As the sea silvers towards evening, and the sun swims through the green gates of the night Elphin notices that there is a leather bag caught on one of the poles of the weir. Together he and the weir-ward take it down and peer inside. The first thing they see is the shining brow of a beautiful child.

"Taliesin!" says Elphin, awed. "He of the radiant brow."

It is not what he had wanted from the day's work at the weir, but it is all that he has to show for it, so he puts the child on his horse and rides with him back to his father's house, sadly wondering what he

will do with another mouth to feed when he has not enough for those already dependent on him.

Softly the child begins to sing, and his voice is sweeter than a maiden's.

> *"Never in Gwyddno's weir*
> *Was there such good luck as this night…*
> *In the day of trouble I shall be to thee*
> *of more service than three hundred salmon!*
> *The miracles of God come unexpectedly*
> *and though I am little I am gifted mightily."*

Elphin looks with astonishment at the child.

"Are you man or spirit?" he asks.

The child sings again. He sings of Caridwen's Cauldron, of the three drops that gave him supernatural sight. He sings of the hunt and the hunted, of being animal, fish, bird and seed that he might learn their wisdom. He sings of the dark months in the earthwomb and of his second birth: he sings of the ocean and of his third birth from its depths: he sings of the joy he will bring to Elphin his friend and of the wisdom he will bring to all who will listen to his words.

"What is this?" says Gwyddno, sternly looking at the leather bag and the child.

"A bard," Elphin says proudly. "My gift from the weir."

"What profit will he bring you?"

"He will bring him more profit than the weir has ever brought you!" says the child.

"Are you able to speak, and you so little?" gasps Gwyddno.

"I am better able to speak than you to question me!" replies the child.

Then Taliesin sings of matters great and small, of past and future, of God and Man. When he is tired Elphin gives him lovingly into the arms of his wife, who tends him as though he were her own.

When Taliesin is thirteen years old his foster father Elphin is invited to the court of the high King, his uncle Maelgwn Gwynedd. He does not go willingly for he knows the reputation of the man. But, because of this very reputation, he knows he dare not refuse the invitation. Since Taliesin's arrival Elphin's confidence has grown, and he is no longer looked upon as ill-favoured and ill-fortuned. His wife is beautiful and virtuous, his home well-appointed and respected. But the High King's castle is a hundredfold larger and a thousand times more richly furnished: his wife more beautiful: his retainers better clad.

Something of Elphin's old awkwardness returns as he listens to the praises of all who are gathered at the High King's bidding. They vie with each other in flattery of Maelgwn Gwynedd. His queen is praised beyond any woman in the kingdom, he has the bravest men, the swiftest horses and greyhounds, the most skilful and the wisest bard. Elphin listens and can no longer hold his tongue. He knows what he knows about the king and his wife and he mutters to those he is nearest that his own wife is more virtuous than the queen and his own bard more inspired than any of the twenty four attending the High King's court. The impertinence of this is reported at once, and Elphin is thrown into prison while the king challenges his double boast.

In chains Elphin bemoans his carelessness of tongue, and fears that the bad luck that dogged him as a youth is about to return.

But at his home Taliesin can see what has occurred in the castle of Dyganwy, and has knowledge of the approach of Rhun, son of Maelgwn. He knows he has been sent by his father to try the virtue of Elphin's wife, and he knows the nature of Maelgwn and Rhun. The boy is aware that they will not use fair means to test the Lady Creirwy.

"Trick to trick we must play my lady," he tells her, and together they array her maid in clothes no maid ever wore, decking her with jewels, combing her hair with silver combs.

"Ah," sighs Rhun, seeing the maid. "Your husband did well to boast of you my lady. Your beauty is astonishing. I am your slave." He bows low and kisses her hand. She bids him rise with a regal gesture her mistress taught her, careful not to speak. Rhun is feasted, minstrels harp and poets sing. Taliesin and the true mistress of the house stay well out of sight.

The first night the maid manages to fend off the opportuning prince of Gwynedd, though he is handsome and auburn haired. On the second night of feasting he slips powder into her mead and she falls easily into his arms. He carries her to Elphin's chamber and there, throughout the long night, he enjoys her.

Before the dawn he cuts off her finger with Elphin's signet ring, and returns to his father, delighted with his success.

Ah, Rhun, prince of Gwynedd, what will become of you if you cannot tell illusion from reality?

The king, triumphant, draws Elphin from his cell, and confronts him with the finger and the ring, telling him that his wife's virtue has been easily overcome by Rhun.

Not so easily deluded, Elphin admits the ring is his ring, but denies that the finger is his wife's.

"Three proofs I will give you, my lord, that this is not my wife's finger. The first is that my wife's thumb is too slender to hold the ring I gave her and yet you see the joint of this little finger holds it firm. The second is that my wife keeps her nails pared and fine week by week, yet this nail has not been attended for a month or more. The third and last proof I will offer you is that this finger shows evidence of kneading rye dough within three days of its being cut off. My wife has never kneaded rye dough since being my wife."

King Maelgwn is angry and throws him back into prison, saying he will test his other boast, the wisdom of his bard.

Taliesin leaves his lady, promising that he will set Elphin free.

He rides to Castle Dyganwy through snow and sleet and wind, and comes to the Great Hall where the fires and feasting are.

He creeps in unannounced, and sits quietly in a corner, biding his time, watching with amusement how little men are puffed up and rogues covered with honours.

At last the moment comes for the heralds and the bards to move forward for the praise-songs and the proclamations. As they sweep past the corner where the boy crouches, in their long furred robes, he blows out his lips at them and plays "blerwm blerwm" with his fingers at them. Some cast angry glances at the unmannerly boy with his shock of golden hair and his impish face, others ignore him.

Trumpets are sounded and the first bard moves into position before the king. The hall falls silent. Heinen Vardd is famous in the valleys for his re-sounding voice and mighty words. The king settles to listen, already anticipating the pleasure of what he is about to hear. He will be praised for his riches, the size of his castle, the number and strength of his men-at-arms, he will he praised for his wife's beauty and the size of the dowry she brought with her, he will be praised for the number of strong men he has killed in single combat, for the armies he has defeated and the dead he has left in the field, for the vengeance he has wrought on any who have crossed him, he will be praised for the speed with which he can down his ale, for the size of the steer turning on the spit, for his lineage, for his ancestors who fought other men's ancestors and killed and killed until he, Maelgwn, High King of High Kings sits where he sits.

Heinen Vardd raises his arm and takes the stance of a man about to launch into a mighty praise-song. And from his lips comes… nothing but the insulting sound of "blerwm blerwm".

Horrified, he stops and tries again. The court listens, frozen, shocked. Again, the foolish sound. The king frowns and orders him to step down. The next bard takes his place, but he fares no better. Angrily the king calls one after the other and as each can say no more than the one before, the king's rage knows no bounds. He strikes Heinen Vardd upon the head, swearing that he will have no drunken brawling bards to serve him at his court. The blow brings the bard to his senses and he speaks clearly at last, telling the king they have been bewitched by the spirit that sits in the corner in the guise of a young boy.

Taliesin is sent for, and stands at last before the king.

"Who are you?" he demands, "and from whence have you come?"

Taliesin, in a voice as sweet as silver, sings his song.

"I am a wonder whose origin is not known.
I was little Gwion
but am now Taliesin.
From the womb of Caridwen I came
From her Cauldron I drew my strength.
And now I am chief bard to Elphin
soon to be chief bard of the West.
Before the world was
I was with my Lord in the highest sphere.
With the fall of Lucifer
I entered Hell.
In the Vale of Hebron
I walked with the Divine Spirit.
In Canaan I witnessed
the death of Absalom.
I was mentor
to Enoch and Elias,

friend to Melchisadek.
At Golgotha my wings were spread,
In Arianrod's prison I have been
and in the ark with Noah and his beasts.
I have seen
the destruction of Sodom and Gomorra
and the destruction yet to come.
No one knows me
yet all have heard my song.
I am neither flesh nor fish
yet all of this
and none.
I was one
and am now another.
I am Taliesin."

Filled with wonder King Maelgwn set his twenty-four bards to compete with him, but none could match his skill.

Taliesin sang on and on. He sang of vengeance as though it were a thing of shame… no man need avenge himself, for each deed brings its own reward, he said. He told the king, not as curse but as warning, that what he had done, and would still do, would bring destruction to himself and all his house…

"a strong creature from before the flood
without flesh, without bone,
without vein, without blood,
without head, without feet…
neither younger, nor older
than the beginning…"

would bring about his doom. He saw what the king could not see: the yellow plague creeping like a bodiless miasma from the rotting, unburied corpses of a future battlefield.

His words chilled the blood of all who heard them and a storm wind shook the castle as though it would shake it down. The king, shivering, called for Elphin to be brought before him.

Taliesin's song became sweet again and the words of praise to his lord Elphin for his kindness, his gentleness, his care of those who needed care, loosened the fetters on his ankles and freed him from all constraint.

Then the boy turned his back on the king and sang directly to the bards, calling them crows that were destroying the harvest of the true poets… warning them that the words they used had power for life and death, yet they used them with no understanding of what was true or what was false, what was to be praised, and what was not to be praised…

Beside the lake of Tegid the Lady Caridwen lived on, her son Avagddu at her side ugly and misshapen and shunned by men, loved and cherished only by her.

One day when he had reached the age of eighteen, he strayed from his usual haunts and came on a place where, if he was cautious, he could he among the rocks and look down upon a village. He could watch unseen the herd boys whistling to the cattle on their way to and from the pastures, the smith at his furnace, the women grinding corn. He noticed in particular a young girl who never seemed to be with the other young girls as they walked, chattering, to the stream to fetch water, but was always a little way behind dreaming, by herself. He began to dream too: seeing himself in his dreams as handsome as the village youths – no, handsomer! He dreamed of coming from his hiding place and walking up the path to meet her, casually greeting her and she, astonished by his beauty, turning her head to gaze admiringly after him as he walked on. In his dream it was she who sought him, coming to his mother's house, pleading for his friendship.

He never told his mother where he went on these summer mornings, but kept it to himself, his secret life the only thing he had ever possessed that was of any great value to him.

After a while he began to leave presents for the maiden. First she found a lark's egg beside the path and carried it tenderly home to hatch. Of an evening when she was spinning she would listen to it sing. All the songs it sang were of the love of Avagddu for Gwendoline – and, Gwendoline was her name. She enquired of everyone in the village who Avagddu might be, but none had heard of him.

One day there was a necklace of fine glass beads, as blue as heaven; another day a tiny shell, a perfect spiral. Flowers were left that did not grow in her valley, and at last a cup carved from clear rock crystal containing mountain water that renewed itself as soon as it was drunk.

The other girls, when they heard of the gifts, sought them for themselves, but found nothing. Only Gwendoline, when she was walking alone, spied them beside the path. Secretly she dreamed of the man who left her the gifts, clothed him in the fine clothes and handsome features of a knight, and dreamed of riding off with him to King Arthur's court…

So the two dreamers dreamed, and never once confronted the reality behind their dreams.

One day the Lady Creirwy asked Taliesin to accompany her to her mother's home and the youth agreed, though, knowing who she was, he wondered if his welcome would be harsh: his foster-mother was the daughter of the Lady Caridwen, and Avagddu, whom he had robbed, was her younger brother. For love of Elphin and because her own heart was clear and kind, the Lady Creirwy had never once held this against her foster son. "What will be, will be," she often said, and took his good fortune as a gift from God, her own brother no doubt having another destiny to fulfil.

As they came into the village where Gwendoline lived, the girl was at the door of her home and spied the great Lady and her companion, the shining headed youth. She was sure that he was the one who had been leaving her presents: he was everything she had ever dreamed about, everything she had ever longed for. It is true he did not greet her, but then their friendship was a secret between them, and he, no doubt, still did not wish to reveal his identity. The girl slipped back into the house and fetched her cloak. Then hurrying she set off to follow the couple, taking care always to remain just out of sight.

After a few hours of this the company chanced to

pass through a forest, on the other side of which lay the lake of Tegid and the home of Caridwen. For a moment Gwendoline lost sight of the travellers among the thick trees and looked around herself, afraid, wondering which path of the two facing her she should take.

She heard a movement on the left hand path and decided that the couple she was following must surely have gone that way. She set off as quickly as she could, deciding that this time she would confront the youth and ask to join them whither they would be going. Night was not far off, and she knew she would not be able to return home easily by herself.

A sound to the side of her made her spin anxiously. From the shadows of the forest a wild boar was watching her, his tusks gleaming cruelly. She stopped at once, her heart pounding, too afraid to call for help, now not so sure she had taken the same path as the travellers, wondering if the boar was what she had heard ahead of her.

A sound from the other side of her made her turn her head in terror, to meet the eyes of a man so ugly and misshapen that there was not much to choose between the two of them: the boar at least was more natural.

Trembling, she could think of nothing to do but pray.

The man stepped forward; the boar lowered its head apparently for the charge.

Oh, why did not her golden haired knight appear and rescue her! Where was he, the giver of gifts and dreams?

Avagddu crashed clumsily through the under-growth and put himself between her and the boar. The girl shut her eyes and held her breath, waiting for the sound of tusk on tearing flesh, the scream of agony. But it did not come. She opened one eye cau-tiously, and saw that the man and boar were staring at each other almost eye to eye, and that the boar was turning away at last with a grunt, almost of ac-knowledgement.

Astonished she stared, wondering what kind of man he was who could do such a deed and whether now the boar was gone she would be in any danger from the man. But before she could complete the thought, he was gone, shambling off into the un-dergrowth, soon out of sight.

She began to run along the path, calling as she ran, desperate now to find the shining youth and his gentle faced mother.

At the home of Caridwen, Taliesin and the Lady Creirwy had arrived and were greeted warmly. Elphin's wife did not tell her mother who Taliesin was, and the Lady did not guess. Warm broth was served, and lanterns lit, shadows gathering fast on the forest and over the waters of the lake.

Creirwy asked after her youngest brother, and was told that as soon as he smelled the broth he would appear.

"He wanders off by himself most of the time," his mother said, "but never far from home. Hunger brings him back."

Taliesin with his Sight could see the girl wander-ing in the forest, the misshapen youth guarding her, he could see the love between them though she at least was unaware of it. He said nothing, for to do so would reveal himself to Caridwen.

They were on their second bowl of broth when at last they heard the plaintive cry of the girl. Caridwen went to the door at once and drew her in, shivering and exhausted, and set her by the hearth to warm.

Shortly after, Avagddu crept in and sat in a dark corner, unseen by her.

When she had drunk some warm milk and eaten a fresh crust of bread, colour returned to her cheeks and she was prepared to tell them her name and from whence she had come. When asked why she had strayed so far from home she would not reply but looked at Taliesin shyly, flushing prettily. The two older women could see at once that Taliesin was the lodestone that had drawn her here, but he seemed unconcerned, apparently unaware of the effect he was having on her.

Later, when mother and daughter had retired to talk and left the three young people alone, Gwendoline charged Taliesin with cold-heartedness in not acknowledging his part in their relationship, thus causing her to look foolish in the women's eyes.

"What part?" he asked.

"What part indeed!" she chided. "The presents… the lark's egg, the necklace – see, I wear it around my neck! – the shell, the crystal cup…"

"I know of no such presents," he said firmly, but in his heart a great sorrow was building its nest. He had fallen in love with the beautiful girl and yearned for her, but with his seeing Eye, which had

become for him over the years something of a curse, he saw that she was beloved of Avagddu and his conscience would not let him rob the young man yet again.

"You do indeed!" she laughed.

"I do not," he replied.

At last a doubt began to grow in the young girl's heart that perhaps she had been mistaken. She hung her head, full of shame.

Taliesin, feeling the suffering of Avagddu, gently drew him forward.

"This is my friend, my brother, Avagddu. It is he who gave the presents you speak of."

The girl looked up and for the first time in the house looked squarely at the ugly youth. Her expression of shock and disappointment was plain to see. Without a word he slipped from the room and was gone into the night.

Then Taliesin the bard began to sing. He sang of forests full of shining trees drawing strength from the earth through gnarled and twisted roots, he sang of plain kindling from which the bright splendour of the flame arises. He sang of the heart that is a bag of blood yet gives the sweetest feelings. He wove such magic with his words that the girl began to see beyond the appearance of things to their real nature, and beneath the ugly shell of Avagddu the kind and gentle man, friend of animals and plants, giver of thoughtful and precious gifts.

Then Taliesin sang of himself – how he could never rest in the present for he could always see what was yet to be, how he could never love because he could read the thoughts of all he loved, how he could never be loved because all feared his Sight.

The young girl wept and slept, and wept again… and in the morning asked Taliesin to find her love and bring him to her. That he did.

And with the marriage of Avagddu and Gwendoline the Lady Caridwen finally forgave Taliesin.

The Twins Of The Tylwyth Teg

The girl dancing and the girl watching from the shadows were two images of beauty identical in every particular. They were twins born to the royal couple on a night when the reflection of the new moon dancing on the lake had seemed to be two images, two faint silver sickles moving on the rippling surface of the black water.

"Look brother," the owl had whispered to his companion, "look what the wind is doing. He has separated the two sides of the moon. No good will come of it."

A dryad had overheard him, looked, and then silently stolen away to spread the word among his friends. Soon the lake had been ringed with elf folk, tree folk, dryads and nymphs, even the old hobgoblin that everyone feared. He laughed to think of the mischief the wind had caused by splitting the image of the new moon like that. He laughed and laughed until the sun had come up and caught him still by the shore alone, exposed, in danger of being seen by the shepherds and herd boys who were driving their sheep and their cattle out to pasture.

But that was long, long ago by human count, a dozen mortal kings had risen to power and fallen to dust since then. But under the lake in the shining palace of the Tylwyth Teg the twin princesses who had been born that night had aged no more than sixteen years.

"Come my child," said the king to the dancing girl, holding out his hand to her. "Come forward, the prince my friend has something for you."

She glided forward and made a curtsy before the handsome young prince who was visiting from the Kingdom of the shining Tor, which was far away on the other side of the Black Mountains where the lakes were even deeper and even richer in darting trout.

"The Princess Haelwyn," the king said. "My daughter."

"No father," the young girl said quickly, looking up, a faint shadow on her brow. "My name is Olwen, Sir," she said to the prince.

"What? A father not knowing the name of his own daughter!" Prince Llewellyn laughed. "If she were mine Sir, there would be nothing about her I would ever forget!" And he looked with admiration at the slender figure, the long tresses that shone like the gold of sunlight on water. Suddenly he blinked and rubbed his eyes. Before him he saw two images of the same girl, both looking at him, smiling.

The King laughed.

"No, you are not insane, my lord. There are two princesses before you, Haelwyn and Olwen."

The prince looked from one to the other, confused.

He had removed a ring from his left hand proposing to give it to the girl who had so pleased him with her dance; but now he could not tell which one she was. One of the girls stepped forward.

"My lord, it pleases me that you enjoyed my dance," she said. He looked into her eyes and was overwhelmed by the deep, rich blue of them, the dark lashes, the soft pink of her cheek. He held out his hands to her and took both her hands in his.

"Lady," he said softly, scarcely above a whisper, "I have never seen such a dance or such a dancer. Will you walk with me and listen while I tell you of my home and all that I desire for it?" He had no eyes for the other girl now, and her face fell.

As her sister and the prince walked away from her, tears came to Olwen's eyes and she turned and ran from the hall.

Haelwyn's jealousy had spoiled things for her before.

One day when Gareth, the son of the widow Gwyneth, was eighteen, he was sitting on a rock beside the lake eating his lunch and waiting for his mother's cattle to munch their fill of the rich grass at the waters edge. He and they had wandered a good way from their usual grazing ground and were enjoying the change of scene. The sun was warming the back of his neck nicely and making him feel peaceful and content. The lake was so still the mountains on the other side were reflected perfectly, as though in a mirror. A cormorant stalked a fish daintily; a moorhen dived and bobbed up again a long way from where it had disappeared.

Gareth's mother had given him barley bread and cheese for lunch and he bit into it with relish. He and the cows had climbed a steep slope to reach the lake and were hungry. He began to think of a song

he would sing when he had finished chewing.

Suddenly his eyes fell on something he had not noticed before. He had been so busy gazing across the lake that he had not noticed a shape to the side not far from him. At first he thought it was a rock, but then he realised that it was a girl. He stared in astonishment. He could see now quite clearly that it was a girl. She must have been sitting on a rock low against the surface of the lake, for she seemed to be at water level and yet not wet at all. She was leaning over, looking at herself in the still water and combing her long hair.

Gareth stood up, holding his breath, and moved very quietly towards her. As he drew nearer he could tell that she was extremely beautiful, unlike any girl he had ever seen before. The girls of the village were buxom and rosy and many a one had he kissed, but their hair was coarse and dark, and hers was like spun sunlight and the satin of a butterfly's wing.

His heart beat very fast. How should he attract her attention? She was so delicately beautiful to shout in a great rough voice would have been quite wrong.

Ah, but she was beautiful!

The song he had been planning fled, and another took its place. Just at that moment, as though she had heard the new song in his heart before he had uttered a note, she turned towards him. Startled, she paused with the comb held above her head. They looked into each other's eyes and it would have been difficult to tell which one was more in awe of the other. The young man was the first to move. He reached forward, his hand full of barley bread and cheese, and said in an embarrassed, awkward voice: "Would you like some bread?"

She looked at his strong brown hand and the crusty brown bread in it. She shook her head very slightly, and said in a voice so soft, so fine, so melodious that the sentence she spoke was almost a song in itself. "Hard baked bread," she said, "is not for me."

And even as her words reached him she began to slide into the still, silver water, and, before his very eyes, disappeared.

Frantically Gareth rushed up and down the shore. He even plunged into the water and searched where she had been but there was no sign of her.

At last, when the long shadows were beginning to creep down the mountain he thought of his mother, and realised that he must get their cattle safely home before nightfall. He found his mother at the cottage door anxiously watching out for him.

"Gareth! Gareth!" she called. "Where have you been? I was worried."

That night he told her all that he had seen and asked her what she thought it could mean. She thought about it a long time over her spinning and then she told him that she thought the girl must be a faery from the lake. When she heard how fine and beautiful the girl was, and how much her son already loved her and longed for her, she thought it would be no bad thing to have a member of the Tylwyth Teg in the family, and advised him to take unbaked bread the next day, seeing that she had not liked the hard, crusty bread.

Long before the sun was up, Gareth was driving

his cows towards the lake. There was no sign of her, but he remembered that he had only seen her at midday the day before, and so he did not lose heart.

But midday came and went and there was still no sign of her. Gareth was so distracted, pacing up and down and searching everywhere for her, that he completely forgot his cows, and when the afternoon was far advanced he suddenly realised that they were nowhere near him. Horrified, he rushed about, calling them by name.

At last he spotted them almost on the other side of the lake, browsing on the very edge of a cliff. "Oh, no!" he gasped, and ran as hard as he could over the rocky ground, in and out of the bracken and the thorny brambles. Panting, he reached them at last, and managed to lead them away from the cliff and down to lower ground.

It was late. The sun was setting, and the still surface of the lake was like mother-of-pearl, the mountains, tinged pale pink, reflecting in the water, the air so still and pure a linnet's call would have sounded harsh. He stood by the lake trembling from his exertion, calming himself by drinking in the beauty of the evening, trying not to feel disappointment that he had not seen the girl again.

A fish leapt, and a circle of ripples travelled out from the point where it had dived again.

He heard another leap to the side, and turned his head towards the sound.

He found the girl, standing quietly in the water, looking shyly at him.

At first he could not move he was so overwhelmed with the joy of finding her. At last he took courage as she showed no sign of leaving, and stepped forward, holding out the unbaked bread he had kept for her.

This time he said nothing.

She looked at the strong brown hand and the unbaked bread and shook her head. "Unbaked bread is not for me," she said softly, and began to sink into the water again.

Gareth's heart nearly broke as he saw her go, but he did not cry out.

Later, when he was walking home remembering every detail of the incident, he could have sworn that there was as much longing in the girl's eyes for him as there was in his for her.

Beneath the waters of the lake when the mountains of the upper earth were dark with night, a party was being held to celebrate the betrothal of the Princess Olwen to Prince Llewellyn of the Shining Tor. The announcement had been made, the guests assembled, when Princess Olwen herself appeared before the throne of her father and the golden chair of his guest to announce that it was not she, Olwen, who had been walking and talking with the prince, but her sister Haelwyn, and that it was therefore Haelwyn who should be betrothed to the prince and not herself.

Two red spots began to appear on the young prince's face.

"Was it not Olwen who danced for me so sweetly?"

"Yes my lord."

"Then it is Olwen that I wish to marry," he said firmly.

Haelwyn had swept into the hall just in time to hear these words.

"My lord," she cried, "it is Olwen you will marry. It is I, Olwen, who danced for you, and I, Olwen, who walked and talked with you."

The King and the prince looked from one young princess to the other. It was impossible to tell which one of the two girls was telling the truth. Slender and beautiful they stood together, river pearls in their golden hair, river pearls round their throats and twining round their arms.

Olwen stood back and bowed to her sister. But there was something in the humility and resignation with which she bowed, something in the gracefulness of her movement, that stirred the prince's heart towards her and not towards her sister Haelwyn, who stood so haughtily proud and straight.

"I think, my lord," the prince said to the king, "it is this princess I wish to marry," and he stepped forward and took Olwen's hand.

She shrank back slightly, thinking of the dark and handsome young man she had seen beside the lake.

Haelwyn's eyes flashed angrily.

"Father!" she cried, "it is I who wear his ring. See!" And she held it out for all to see. The prince was troubled. It was undoubtedly his ring – but there was something in the manner of the girl who wore it he did not like though she was in every possible physical particular identical with the other.

Now Olwen spoke up.

"Father," she said, "it is my sister who should wed the prince. It is she who loves him. I for my part am in love with a mortal man and can give my heart to no other."

This announcement caused a stir in the halls of the Tylwyth Teg. Everyone crowded round: everyone spoke at once. Ever since his wife had moved on to a different realm of Being, the king had brought up the two girls by himself. He loved them dearly and saw no difference in them. For one to marry the prince of the Shining Tor was a great honour, and he had planned another such honour for the other. But a mortal man! That must never be. Mortal men experienced hardships unknown to the Tylwyth Teg. His beautiful daughter would grow old and wrinkled as mortal women did and bear children in suffering.

"No!" he cried. "Daughter, what can you be thinking of?"

Haelwyn smiled. She saw a way at last of being herself, unique as others were unique, her sister's image, now so disturbingly echoing every feature of her own, changed by mortal travail to something very different from her own.

"Father," she said cunningly, "if Haelwyn loves this mortal, would you deny her happiness by denying her his company? For shame! Where is your love – your care – your promise to our mother that our happiness would come before anything else with you?"

"But happiness with a mortal fades as quickly as a dew drop in the sun! Their lives are so short that we scarcely blink while one of their years passes."

"Such a moment as the dew drop knows I would cherish more than all the years in our kingdom, my father," Olwen said. "A dew drop shines in the sun for its brief moment with a light that is more beautiful and intense than the dim glow of this our lakeland home."

The prince was still looking bewildered from one to the other.

Their father's heart was heavy; but he knew the strength of love. Had he not taken their mother from the sunshine and the flowers to live under water with him, and had she not gladly given up everything for him?

At last it was decided that both girls should be presented to the mortal, and if he chose the right one, the one who was in love with him, he should be allowed to marry her. If he could not tell the difference between them he would never see either of them again.

The prince agreed to this because he knew that the one he had given the ring to could not be the one who loved the mortal, for she had not had time to leave his side. The ring was taken from Haelwyn's finger, and the two princesses were prepared in identical clothes for the test.

On the third day Gareth brought bread that was just lightly baked to the lake, still soft, yet slightly crisp around the edges.

But the whole day passed and he did not see her. Almost at nightfall, when he was sadly leaving, he saw cattle walking on the still waters of the lake and stopped in his tracks, trembling, sure that these were magic beasts and that she could not be far behind. He was right. When more than a score of the cattle had quietly trod the water from one end of the lake to the other he found her walking behind.

This time she sweetly accepted the bread and stood so near him that she could almost hear the beating of his heart. At last he spoke, and asked if she would marry him. To his astonished delight she nodded her golden head and smiled at him. At once he reached out his arms to her, but she held up her fine white hand and he hesitated.

"There have to be conditions," she said softly. "My father will insist."

"Of course!" he cried. "I will do anything."

"I cannot live with you if you strike me."

"Never," he said, shocked at the very thought. "I will love you as no man has ever loved a woman. You will have no cause to fear me."

"My father says I may stay with you until I have received three uncalled for blows – and then you will never see me again."

Gareth laughed. "Then you will stay with me for-ever – for I will never strike you."

He stepped into the water up to his knees and reached out his arms towards her once again. But even as he did so she disappeared and he was alone at the edge of the lake.

He gave a great cry of despair and plunged into the water. His love for her now was so strong that he could not bear to live without her. Water weeds be-gan to cling and tug at his legs and he made no effort to free himself from them.

Suddenly something flashed across the water and Gareth pushed his head once more to the surface, hoping against hope that she had come back. He found himself in the middle of the lake, in the deepest part, standing on the surface as though he were on dry land, and before him were three figures, an old man and two beautiful young girls. Two girls identical to the one he loved! He looked from one to the other with astonishment and dismay.

The old man, silver haired and venerable, began to speak.

"My daughter tells me that you have asked to marry her, mortal," he said, his voice rumbling over the lake like distant thunder on a summer's day.

The young man began to tremble, but he nodded dumbly.

The old man's expression was stern. "I will give my permission," he said, "if you can show me which one of these two maidens it is you love."

Gareth looked from one to the other again, and despaired. There was no difference between them; their long hair was like finest spun gold, their eyes like the deepest heavens, their cheeks, their chins, their limbs... all were identical. His heart began to beat faster. What if he chose the wrong one?

The old man's eyes watching him so penetratingly showed Gareth there would be no compromise. If he did not choose the right one he would lose her forever. There would be no second chance. The very mountains round the lake seemed to gather closer, waiting, listening curiously to know if the young mortal could tell reality from the appearance of things, his true love from her sister. There was no breath of wind, no bird call, no tinkling distant cow bell to disturb the silence in which the girls stood, motionless, identical.

Gareth began to sweat although he felt cold. Fear of losing her began to cloud his vision. His heart cried out for his lovely lady of the lake, remembering the soft shine of her eyes, the shy smile, the subtle but powerful feeling he had had that, in spite of the fact that hardly any words had passed between them, he and she were meant for each other and needed no words to further their love.

He blinked and his vision cleared. That was it! There were other ways of reaching knowledge than by the senses. He would look into her eyes and her soul would speak to his soul and he would know her at once, for no two souls were the same, each individual from the beginning and each standing alone at the end.

He looked into one pair of eyes, ignoring now the rich blue of the iris and the delicate shadowing of the long dark lashes. It was as though he were looking into glass. He could see his own image reflected back at him from the surface.

He looked into the other pair of eyes, again ignoring the physical beauty of what he saw. It was as though he were looking into a deep pool, and every moment that he looked the pool seemed to him to be deeper and deeper, the depths rich with memory and promise.

He stepped forward and reached out his arms to the one he knew he loved, the one whose eyes had shown him the depths of her soul. Her face, which had been so composed and stiff, broke into a beautiful shining smile, and she ran to him. For the first time he held his love in his arms and felt her cool limbs entwined in his.

When at last they looked up Haelwyn had disappeared, but the king of the lake was still beside them.

"You have shown a rare sense of discrimination, young mortal," he said in a voice that was no longer stern, no longer frightening. "You shall have my daughter on the condition she has already given you. She will leave on the instant you strike her a third blow without just cause, and you will never see her again."

Gareth shook his head vigorously. "Have no fear," he cried, "that I will ever strike her. I will love her and cherish her to the end of my days."

"Then take her, mortal, and cherish her and love her to the end of your days, and as dowry take as many of my cattle as she can count in one breath."

Olwen laughed and clapped her hands. She turned and looked across the lake. Grazing on the silver water were the sleek and silky cows of her father's magic herd. She took a deep breath and counted. She counted in fives, and as she counted them the cows moved off the lake. Gareth watched with astonishment as his own herd grew and her father's dwindled. When at last Olwen's breath gave out and she fell into his arms laughing and breathless, he had a sizeable herd, the old man was nowhere to be seen, and the sun was setting behind the Black Mountain.

At the same moment two weddings were celebrated. Beneath the lake Haelwyn, still claiming to be Olwen, was married to the Prince of the Shining Tor, and folk of the Fair Family from the distant hills and valleys and lakes gathered to dance at her

wedding. If any mortal had been beside the lake that evening he would have been startled by the glow the water gave out, as though the full moon had dropped right into the lake and was shining from beneath the surface instead of from the sky. The singing was high and fine, the melody gay and bright. All were happy that the king's two beautiful daughters had found husbands that they loved, and particularly pleased that it was Olwen, whom they all secretly preferred, who was to stay with them in faeryland and Haelwyn, who often made them feel uneasy, who had left to join the mortals. No one suspected that the bride had tricked them all, and was not who she said she was.

No one suspected, not even the bridegroom, until the nuptial knot was safely tied and the bride threw off her shoes and joined in the dance. As she danced, slowly it dawned on the Prince that this was not the girl who had danced before. Her movements had not the liquid grace that had enchanted him, and as she turned and turned he did not think of reed flowers in the wind but of deep, dark whirlpools ready to engulf him.

Above ground the wedding of Gareth and Olwen was less magnificent and it was only the village people who gathered to dance for the young couple. There was no ambrosia served or honey wine, no silver bells to chime out the wedding tune, but the widow Gwyneth had baked the cake with joy and love, and all who tasted it remembered it with pleasure for the rest of their lives, and the singing was the most beautiful ever heard, for, though mor-

tal, the people of the Welsh villages can sing more sweetly than any creature on the earth or under it.

There was much curiosity as to where Gareth had found such a beautiful and elegant wife, but neither Gwyneth nor Gareth, nor Olwen herself, gave away that she was of the Tylwyth Teg, the Fair Family, though many suspected it, especially when she threw off her shoes and danced, for no mortal girl had ever trod so lightly or moved so fleetly.

As the years went by Gareth and Olwen prospered in every way. Their love was good and they were given the pleasure of children, three sons as handsome as their father and as gentle as their mother. When they were not helping their father run the farm, which had now grown to a fair size with the help of the magic cattle Olwen had brought with her, they were running about in the hills and down to the lake with their mother. She taught them things no mortal boys were ever taught.

One day a friend of theirs in a neighbouring village was having her new born baby christened and Gareth and his family were invited. As it happened they were so busy on the farm that they found when they came to get ready to go they had hardly left themselves enough time for the travelling. Gareth became very agitated and shouted to the boys to get the cart ready while he fetched the horse from the field. The horse, sensing his agitation, shied away from him, tossing its head and galloping to the far corner of the field. Olwen, seeing the predicament her husband was in, offered to catch the horse herself while he ran to the house for her gloves.

When he returned he found her sitting on the stile calmly and dreamily singing. The horse was still in the field. Impatiently he tapped her on the shoulder with her gloves. "What are you doing?" he cried. "This is no time for singing." She gave him a strange, sad look, and with dismay he realised that he had struck her without just cause, for the horse, enchanted by her singing, at that moment came up to her and nuzzled against her knee.

Meanwhile in the hidden kingdom beneath the Shining Tor, Prince Llewellyn had been told he must keep his wife Haelwyn with him until he had given her three surprise gifts freely from his heart and then he would be free of her and she would return to her father's house. This had been pronounced when it was discovered he had married the wrong twin and he had asked to be released from his marriage vows. He had thought at first that this condition would be an easy one to fulfil, but in practice it had not worked out so well. Haelwyn was greedy and asked for so much that there was nothing he could give her she had not already demanded. He was always looking for a way to give her presents and she was always anticipating him by asking for whatever it was before he had the chance to give it.

Time did not pass as fast in the kingdom of the Tylwyth Teg as it did in the mortal one, and Haelwyn had not been married three months when her twin, already the mother of three young boys, received the first of the unjust blows. Now if the two princesses had been placed together there would have been no difficulty in telling them apart: Haelwyn had grown fat with all the good food she had asked for and been given, while Olwen, still slim, had a few grey hairs and wrinkles to show she was no longer as young as she had been.

On the day Olwen and Gareth were late for the christening of their friend's baby, Haelwyn was out riding on her faery steed in the mountains beyond the Shining Tor. The day was hot and she found that after a time she was weary and thirsty and far from home. Her companions had become separated from her and call as she might she could not make them hear. For the first time in her life of indulgent happiness she felt discomfited, and a tear gathered in her eye and started to trickle down her cheek. Even as it did so she noticed a traveller coming along the track ahead of her, on foot, carrying a water jar on his shoulder. He stopped in front of her and his eyes from beneath the brim of his hat surveyed her. He saw that she was tired and that a tear was on her cheek. He felt sorry for her and handed up the water jar for her to drink.

"Thank you," she sighed gratefully.

"In exchange for that tear, lady," he said, "I will give you any directions you may ask for, for I can see you are lost."

"That is easily done, sir," she said, and reached up to her cheek. The stranger took the tear and put it in a small crystal vial that he carried at his belt.

Haelwyn followed his instructions and was soon home. When she rushed in to tell her husband of the traveller who had been so kind to her and had given her a drink of refreshing water without her even asking for it he said nothing, but smiled and held up a small crystal vial in which was one tear drop. Her husband! He had been the stranger on the track! And now he had given her his first surprise gift from the heart. She bit her lip and thought that she must be careful such a thing did not happen again, or she would find herself back in her father's house.

A few more years passed in Olwen's life with Gareth, and their happiness together was even greater than it had been before. One day they were invited to a friend's wedding and the widow Gwyneth, who was old now, sewed Olwen a beautiful dress for the occasion.

The children were left at home in the care of their grandmother, and Gareth and Olwen set off in high spirits. They had not met the bride, but the groom was a very old friend of theirs. The day was bright, the church bells chiming merrily. All went well until the minister began to say the words of the vow for the young couple to repeat after him, and then Olwen started to weep noisily and cry out that they should not say the words. Horrified, Gareth tapped her on the arm and told her to hush. All eyes were on them, and the couple looked upset. Olwen buried her face in her hands and made no further sound. She did not even join in the singing of the hymns at the end.

When they were outside Gareth asked her angrily what she had been thinking of to create such a disturbance. Tears began to fall freely from Olwen's eyes again. "You have struck me once again unjustly my husband. I was weeping for their sorrow, for their marriage will not be blessed as ours has been."

"Hush," he whispered, drawing her away from the crowds, anxious that her gloomy words should not be heard by anyone else to spoil the festivity or the day.

As they drove home in their little cart, both hearts were heavy to think that two of the fatal blows had been struck and that now there was but one between them and parting.

And Olwen had been right: the young couple's love turned to hate, and within two years one had murdered the other.

In the land of the Shining Tor, three months after the first surprise gift, Haelwyn was trapped again.

This time she was ill, and lay on her bed crying with the pain in her stomach. She asked for medicines and was given them, but she did not ask for the rare and beautiful rose that her husband brought to her in pity for her pain.

She was so charmed by it that she forgot she should not accept anything from him she had not asked for, and took it in her hands, raising its rich and glowing petals to her face, sniffing deeply at the musky scent.

Colour began to come back to her cheeks again and the pain was forgotten. Gratefully she looked over the flower and met her husband's eyes. She knew then that she had only one more freely given gift to receive and she would have to leave his court.

After this she was happy no longer, but grew quite thin and pale.

In the mortal world the next few years did not pass as happily as the first ones, for both Gareth and Olwen felt the shadow of parting over them. Gareth was very careful how he touched his wife in case he gave her a blow by mistake.

Their eldest son was nearly fifteen and their youngest nine when Gareth's mother Gwyneth died, bringing sorrow to their hearts, for they both loved her dearly.

At the funeral when the coffin was being slowly and solemnly carried up the aisle and all the villagers stood around weeping in their black clothes Olwen suddenly lifted up her head and started to laugh. Startled, Gareth looked up and struck her on the knee to make her stop, but instead of stopping she leapt up and started to dance around the coffin, singing and laughing and shouting out that they should all be happy and not sad, for Gwyneth had gone to a lovely place, full of joy and peace.

One of the deacons took her by the arm and led her out from amongst the horrified and angry parishioners. Gareth stayed behind the full length of the funeral, his thoughts angry against his unconventional wife for disgracing him in such a way.

Not until the last sod of earth fell on his mother's coffin lid did the full implication of what Olwen had said and what he had done by hitting her knee dawn on him.

With a cry of despair he ran from the grave-side, calling her name.

It was too late.

When Gareth reached home he found no trace of

Olwen, nor of any one of the magic cattle her father had given her as her dowry. Even the calves that had been born to them were gone... even the little dead calf that had been on the spit ready for the funeral feast was gone.

Sadly he walked by the lake calling... asking her forgiveness for his lack of understanding... but the water remained smooth, and the reflection of the mountain was all he could see in the lake.

In the land of the Shining Tor Haelwyn asked for jewels and asked for furs. She asked for a little silver dog and for a golden bird. She asked and asked and her husband could think of nothing to give her that she had not already asked for.

One day, when she was sitting on a pile of things that he had given her, her maidens singing and dancing around her, her musicians playing drums and fifes, she felt desperate and sad. At that moment her husband came into the room and held up his hand. At once all the noise and movement stopped, and a beautiful, restful silence surrounded them. She looked up across the heads of all the people and over the piles of all the things that she possessed and met her husband's eyes.

"My lord, you have won," she said, "for you have given me the greatest gift of all and the one I did not know I needed."

"What is that, princess?"

"A moment of peace and quiet. I thank you, and I will now go back to my father's house, ashamed that I tricked you into marrying me, ashamed that I tried to trick you into keeping me."

Without taking one thing of all that he had given her, she left him and went back to the lake beneath the Black Mountain.

There she found her sister and together they sat and talked over all that had befallen them since they had parted.

Haelwyn felt no more jealousy for her sister, and, although they were still alike, the different experiences they had each had showed in their faces and they no longer mirrored each other.

Together they wept for what they had lost, and together they planned the future. Their father had decided to follow his wife to the shining lands beyond the known realms, and charged them, together, with the ruling of his kingdom.

No kingdom in the land of the Tylwyth Teg was ruled with greater justice than that lake kingdom beneath the Black Mountain of Carmarthenshire. Queen Olwen and Queen Haelwyn kept their youth and their beauty and their friendship with each other as the years sped by among mortals.

The sons of Olwen grew straight and tall and became famous in all the valleys around the Black Mountain for their extraordinary knowledge of herbs, and the mysterious skill with which they healed people of anything that ailed them.

Gareth grew old, proud of his sons, happy in the memories he had of his years with Olwen. Prince Llewellyn took another wife and enjoyed her company, though sometimes for no reason he could think of, he would take out the crystal vial and stare at Haelwyn's tear.

About Moyra Caldecott

Moyra Caldecott was born in Pretoria, South Africa in 1927, and moved to London in 1951. She married Oliver Caldecott and raised three children. She has degrees in English and Philosophy and an M.A. in English Literature.

Moyra Caldecott has earned a reputation as a novelist who writes as vividly about the adventures and experiences to be encountered in the inner realms of the human consciousness as she does about those in the outer physical world. To Moyra, reality is multidimensional.

www.ingramcontent.com/pod-product-compliance
Lightning Source LLC
Chambersburg PA
CBHW050904180626
46814CB00007B/2897